E
ARN
Arnold, Marsha Diane.

The pumpkin runner.

E
ARN
Arnold, Marsha Diane.

The pumpkin runner.

302517

DATE	BORROWER'S NAME	

DISCARD

BAKER & TAYLOR

The Pumpkin Runner

Marsha Diane Arnold / Pictures by Brad Sneed

Dial Books for Young Readers New York

To Cliff Young, the farmer from Victoria who loves to run
—M. D. A.

To Erin and Melissa
—B. S.

Published by Dial Books for Young Readers
A member of Penguin Putnam Inc.
375 Hudson Street
New York, New York 10014

Text copyright © 1998 by Marsha Diane Arnold
Pictures copyright © 1998 by Bradley D. Sneed
All rights reserved
Designed by Nancy R. Leo
Printed in Hong Kong on acid-free paper
First Edition
1 3 5 7 9 10 8 6 4 2

Library of Congress Cataloging in Publication Data
Arnold, Marsha Diane.
The pumpkin runner/by Marsha Diane Arnold; pictures by Brad Sneed.—1st ed.
p.   cm.
Summary: An Australian sheep rancher who eats pumpkins for energy enters
a race from Melbourne to Sydney, despite people laughing at his eccentricities.
ISBN 0-8037-2124-2 (trade)—ISBN 0-8037-2125-0 (lib. bdg.)
[1. Running—Fiction. 2. Pumpkins—Fiction.
3. Australia—Fiction. 4. Individuality—Fiction.]
I. Sneed, Brad, ill. II. Title.
PZ7.A7363Pu 1998 [E]—dc21   97-26666   CIP   AC

The art for this book was prepared using oil paints on canvas.

Nearly all the sheep ranchers in Blue Gum Valley rode horses or drove jeeps to check on their sheep. But Joshua Summerhayes liked to run . . . with Yellow Dog trailing behind him.

Joshua had been running for fifty years, ever since he was ten years old. That was the year his family planted a pumpkin patch behind their clapboard ranch house, where the sun sparkled through the eucalyptus trees near Blue Gum Creek.

When the pumpkins had grown as round as a wombat's belly, young Joshua stopped by to enjoy a golden slice. He felt such an energy from the sun-filled pumpkin that he pulled on his orange gumboots, shuffled a dance in the dusty earth, and took off running . . . with the great-great-great-grandfather of Yellow Dog trailing behind. That day he ran forty kilometers, all the way to Cockatoo Canyon, just to check on a newborn lamb.

"Must be the way the sun shines through the eucalyptus trees that gives the pumpkins that extra spark," Aunt Millie had said as she watched Joshua's dust trail.

Now Joshua was getting up in years, and every January at the Sheep Ranchers' Woolly Boolly Barbecue the ranchers teased him. "You're getting mighty old to be running all over a ten-thousand-acre sheep ranch," said Rancher Waudley. "When are you going to buy a jeep?"

Joshua smiled and shuffled his gumboots in the dust. "I like to run," he said.

"As long as he's got pumpkins to eat, he'll keep running," added Aunt Millie.

One day Joshua and Yellow Dog were resting on the porch after a long run over to Bandicoot Creek, when the wind blew a newspaper—SMACK—into Joshua's face. When he opened his eyes, he read:

☞ **12th ANNUAL KOALA-K RACE** ☜

900 KILOMETERS
FROM MELBOURNE TO SYDNEY

MAY 4th

$10,000 PRIZE

"It's been a while since we've visited the city, Yellow Dog," Joshua said. "We could see two cities and get in a little run as well."

Yellow Dog thumped his tail against the wooden porch-planks.

Joshua packed a clean pair of overalls and his newest pair of gumboots for the run. Rancher Waudley offered his jeep for the trip.

"Mighty grateful, mate," said Joshua, piling the last pumpkin from his patch into the jeep as Aunt Millie loaded her cooking tools. "Not sure I could carry all the pumpkins I'll need for a nine-hundred-kilometer run."

The morning was still dark when Joshua pulled up to the runners' registration table in Melbourne. Mr. Manning, the race official, looked over his glasses at the lanky man driving the jeep, the yellow dog sitting beside him, and the old woman snoring atop a pile of pumpkins.

"You sure you're in the right place?" he asked.

"If this is the Koala-K," answered Joshua. "I've come to run."

Wanting to be friendly, Joshua and Yellow Dog introduced them-
selves to the eight other runners while Aunt Millie got a few more
winks.

"I've run two hundred kilometers a week for three months training for this race," said Damien Dodgerelle, raising one eyebrow at Joshua and looking down his long nose at Yellow Dog. "And you?"

"I just check my herds, from sunup to sundown," said Joshua.

"I train every day with three-hundred-pound weights," Damien
continued, doing a one-handed push-up.

"I carry an injured sheep in now and again," Joshua replied.

Reporters pushed Joshua aside as they threw questions at Damien. Word was out he was a shoo-in to win. Joshua was shoved into Katerina Volta, who was gulping down a vial of purple liquid.

"It's my specially formulated energy drink," she explained, "Katerina's Secret Power Punch."

At that moment Mr. Manning stopped by. "We're setting up the food and water stops along the course. What can we take for you, Mr. Summerhayes?"

"That jeep full of pumpkins should do," Joshua answered. "Just give Aunt Millie a map of the course."

As starting time approached, Joshua changed into his fresh pair of overalls and clean boots.

"Nylon shorts and running shoes are the usual attire for a runner," said Mr. Manning, staring at Joshua's orange gumboots.

"These do me on the ranch," Joshua answered. "Guess they'll do me here."

As the sun called up the morning, spectators lined the road. A few of the young ones snickered and giggled at the gray-haired man in overalls and gumboots. Yellow Dog growled softly, but Joshua said, "Never mind now."

Banners flew above the crowd. Peddlers sold sun lotion and sodas. Reporters floated overhead in balloons, snapping photos. The other runners started to flex and stretch. Joshua nibbled a slice of pumpkin.

At two minutes till eight the crowd grew quiet. Banners stopped flying, peddlers stopped selling, balloonists hovered in anticipation.

At precisely 8 A.M. Mr. Manning sounded the starting gun.
Eight runners sped swiftly past the cheering spectators.
Joshua shuffled by waving, while Yellow Dog sniffed the ground to
get his bearings.

As they passed through the city, eight runners looked straight ahead.

Joshua called hello to the rowing crews on the River Yarra. Yellow Dog barked greetings to the trolley passengers.

By afternoon the runners were deep in the countryside and tiring. Except Joshua. He kept pulling a slice of pumpkin from his pocket and chewing on it. He'd give a slice to Yellow Dog and they'd keep shuffling along, steady-like.

By the first stop at Wallaby Ridge, Joshua was running alongside the others. As Katerina Volta gulped her Secret Power Punch, Joshua and Yellow Dog ate Aunt Millie's pumpkin stew. Then Joshua ran off like it was another day on the sheep ranch and he was going to check a mother ewe at Dry Creek Landing.

The third day, word got out that the sheep rancher wearing overalls and gumboots was leading the race. A crowd was at Platypus Pond to cheer him through Aunt Millie's pumpkin soup.

The day after that the news wire told the world about Joshua. Photographers from Paris to Hong Kong were at Wombat Flat to watch Joshua and Yellow Dog enjoy their pumpkin seed pudding.

"Not too many pictures," Joshua said. "Yellow Dog is camera shy."

The world was so busy watching Joshua shuffling along that the other racers were nearly forgotten. But Damien Dodgerelle had not forgotten the $10,000 prize.

When one of the balloons dropped down for repairs, Damien made a deal with the balloonist: half the prize money for a shortcut over Wollongong.

Joshua and Yellow Dog were within twenty kilometers of the finish line when Damien Dodgerelle caught sight of them. "Set me down in front of them, on the other side of that wattle grove," Damien shouted.

Just as the balloon was about to set down, a jeep half-filled with pumpkins roared out of the grove. Aunt Millie had spent all night baking a Pumpkin Victory Cake and she was late for the last stop.

As she swerved to miss the balloon, the balloon swayed to miss her. Damien ended—SMACK—in the middle of mashed pumpkins. Aunt Millie ended—SMACK—in the middle of squashed cake. And the balloon ended—SMACK—on top of the jeep.

When Joshua and Yellow Dog arrived at the last check-in, Aunt Millie and the pumpkins were nowhere to be seen. Yellow Dog sniffed the ground and whimpered. Joshua sat down and pondered what to do without his pumpkin energy.

As the sun sparkled through the eucalyptus trees onto Joshua's head, he felt the energy racing through his body the way it raced through sun-filled pumpkins.

Joshua got up and shuffled a dance in the dusty earth. "Well, now, Yellow Dog, we've come here to run, and that's just what we're going to do. But this last bit of running we'll be doing on our own."

Nearing the finish line, Joshua waved hello to the cheering crowds. The snickering boys and giggling girls were now clapping and jumping up and down. Yellow Dog held his head high.

"Two days and two hours off the record!" Mr. Manning exclaimed, running up with a silver trophy. The crowd squeezed around as Mr. Manning presented Joshua the check for $10,000.

Joshua split the winnings with his fellow runners, even Damien Dodgerelle. He kept only enough for new overalls and gumboots and gave the rest of his share to Rancher Waudley to repair the jeep and to Aunt Millie for new cooking tools.

"Yellow Dog and I just came for the run," he said.

It's been some years since Joshua Summerhayes broke the record in that famous Koala-K Race. These days all the other sheep ranchers in Blue Gum Valley steer four-wheel drives and fly airplanes to check on their sheep.

But Joshua Summerhayes still likes to run . . . with Yellow Dog trailing behind him.

Author's Note

The Pumpkin Runner was inspired by Cliff Young, a 61-year-old farmer from Victoria, Australia, who shuffled from obscurity to national prominence in 1983 when he defeated younger opponents in an 875-kilometer (542-mile) run between Sydney and Melbourne, cutting nearly two days off the record.

He won $10,000 for winning the race, which he split with the other runners.